THIS BOOK BELONGS TO:

....

WHOSE FAVORITE FOOD IS:

....

Tundra Books, an imprint of Penguin Random House Canada Young Readers,
a Penguin Random House Company

Library and Archives Canada Cataloguing in Publication

Garrity-Riley, Kelsey, author, illustrator
    Frankie's favorite food / Kelsey Garrity-Riley.

Issued in print and electronic formats.
ISBN 978-0-7352-6431-1 (hardcover).—ISBN 978-0-7352-6432-8 (EPUB)

    I. Title.

PZ7.1.G37Fra 2019   j813'.6   C2018-905198-1
                                            C2018-905198-1

Published simultaneously in the United States of America by Tundra Books of
Northern New York, an imprint of Penguin Random House Canada Young Readers,
a Penguin Random House Company

Library of Congress Control Number: 2018956784

Acquired by Tara Walker
Edited by Jessica Burgess
Designed by John Martz
The artwork in this book was created using gouache and ink with a tiny bit of colored pencil.
The text was set in Archer.

Printed and bound in China

www.penguinrandomhouse.ca

1   2   3   4   5   23   22   21   20   19

To Collin, who eats everything.

With much love and gratitude also to Erik, Mom, Dad, Eliza, Shannon and Llewyn for all the years behind and ahead of us spent making memories around the table.

Kelsey Garrity-Riley

FRANKIE'S FAVORITE FOOD

tundra

The end-of-the-school-year play was just one day away.

All the kids at Sunview Elementary prepared to dress up as their favorite foods for the show.

Everyone was busy cutting, gluing and painting.

Everyone but Frankie, that is.

It's not that Frankie was a picky eater.

The problem was that he liked *everything*.

He couldn't possibly choose just one favorite food.

How could he decide between a bowl of chowder and some fresh guacamole?

Or pick between a strawberry tart and a mozzarella salad?

Maybe Frankie could mix together some of his favorites . . .

"Can I be pancakes topped with tomato soup and sprinkled with popcorn?"

"I'm not sure that's a real dish."

"Or a plate of nachos with spring rolls and marzipan on top?"

"Can we simplify that a bit, Frankie?"

"How about a fishstick, olive, pad thai, parmesan, kimchi, couscous, pickle, hummus and cheesecake sandwich?"

"Oh dear."

On the day of the show, the school halls buzzed with excitement.

Frankie had stayed up past his bedtime thinking and thinking, but he still couldn't figure out what food to be.

Thankfully, Ms. Mellon had a great idea.

"Frankie, since you're so excited about *all* the foods, maybe you could be the costume manager? We could use your expertise!"

Frankie was happy with his special job —
everyone looked so delicious! He set to work
helping his classmates get into their costumes
and making sure they
looked their freshest.

Ms. Mellon stood up to start the program.

"Welcome to this year's Sunview Elementary Foodstravaganza!" she said. "Everyone, please hold your applause until the end."

Frankie added some last-minute garnishes backstage.

The show started off with a balanced breakfast.

Frankie was very proud of how the bacon sizzled.

"You're doing an EGGcellent job!" whispered Frankie.

Then the Snack Pack sang some songs.

Next on stage were the preschoolers,
who needed a little extra help serving up
their rice and beans.

Billy got so carried away trying to break dance in his burrito costume, he accidentally rolled offstage.

"Oh no! My salsa!"

The cheeses were perfectly cheesy.

"GOUDA job, guys!" cheered Frankie.

"It's the FALAFEL of the Opera!"

"It's a PITA that song wasn't longer."

Some corny jokes got the audience laughing.

The peas snapped along with a little beet-boxing.

Farfalle did
the foxtrot.

Tortellini tangoed.

Margot twirled so fast,
some of her macaroni flew off.

And the dance of the dumplings was really something.

While a bunch of fruits belted out their song, Frankie sang along from backstage.

And he was ready to
help in case anyone
forgot their lines.

Finally, a group
of desserts closed
out the show.

"Heeey
MACARON-a!"

Frankie happily cleaned up backstage.
His classmates had done so well!

He looked down at all the bits and pieces
he was sweeping up.

Suddenly he had an idea!

Frankie ran around
grabbing up scraps.

Some papier-mâché pasta here,
a few plastic beans there.

He had discovered the one costume that combined all his favorite foods . . .